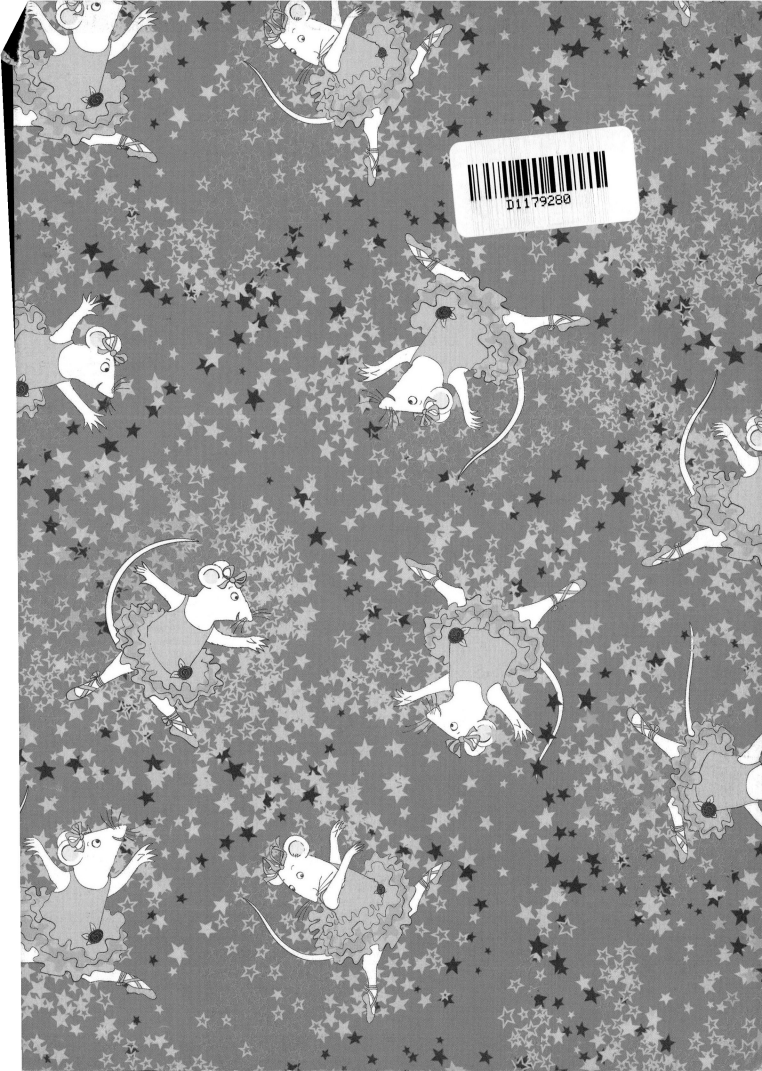

Angelina Ballerina – Princess Dance

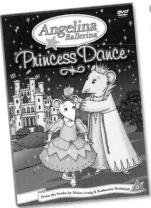

Catch Angelina in this magical fairy-tale adventure – never seen on TV! In this special feature-length edition, Angelina cannot believe her ears to learn that Queen Seraphina has invited her to direct a special mouselings' performance of "Sleeping Beauty" at the Palace. The Queen wants her two daughters to be in the show and Angelina, presuming that as they are princesses they must be talented, gives them starring roles! However, Angelina soon discovers that they are in fact terrible dancers and the performance seems doomed … can Angelina save the show?

To find out, look out for Angelina's DVD from November 2005.

A perfect gift for a little star!

For further information go to www.angelinaballerina.com

This Angelina Ballerina Annual belongs to

Angelina Ballerina™

Annual 2006

Contents

Based on the text by Katharine Holabird
Illustrations by Helen Craig

Angelina, Angelina Ballerina, and the Dancing Angelina logo are trademarks of HIT Entertainment PLC, Katharine Holabird and Helen Craig Ltd. Angelina is registered in the UK and Japan and with the US Patent and Trademark Office. The Dancing Angelina logo is registered in the UK.

EGMONT
We bring stories to life

Published in Great Britain in 2005 by Egmont Books Limited, 239 Kensington High Street, London W8 6SA.
All rights reserved. Printed in Italy. ISBN 1 4052 2042 2
3 5 7 9 10 8 6 4

Hello!

I really hope you enjoy my new annual!
You can read all about me and my friends, my family, my dance teacher Miss Lilly – and, of course, about ballet!

Angelina

Meet me and my family

We're the Mouseling family. We live in Mouseland in an old cottage in a village called Chipping Cheddar. There are houses, shops and a school — but the best place of all is the ballet school.

I'm Angelina Mouseling, and I just love to dance. I may be a little mouse, but I have a big, big dream. I know it will take lots of hard work, but I'm going to be a star ballerina one day — just you wait and see!

This is Matilda Mouseling — my mum. She's a great cook and she sews lovely ballet costumes for me to wear. But best of all, she's always there when I need her.

I just love being a big sister because my baby sister Polly is so cute. She can't talk yet, but somehow I always know just what she's trying to say!

My dad's name is Maurice. He owns the local paper, the Mouseland Gazette, and when he's not working there he loves playing his fiddle. He enjoys jokes, too.

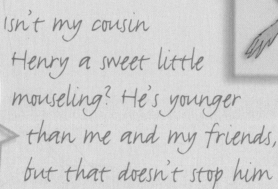

Isn't my cousin Henry a sweet little mouseling? He's younger than me and my friends, but that doesn't stop him enjoying our adventures.

Grandpa and Grandma live in the next village and I love it when they come to visit, especially when Grandpa has an exciting new story to tell me.

Meet my friends — and enemies!

My very best friend in all the world is called Alice Nimbletoes. She's always ready to laugh at just about anything — when she hasn't got her head stuck in a book or her paw in a bag of cheesy nibbles!

Miss Lilly is just — wonderful! She's my dance teacher, and my hero, too. I want to be just like her when I grow up. That means I'm going to be a famous ballerina!

Sammy is a bit older than me, and he's always doing something naughty, so he's a lot of fun! He's very sporty, and doesn't think much of ballet, but I don't care!

William Longtail is sweet and kind. Some of the boy mouselings make fun of him because he dances, but that's one of reasons I like him.

Mrs Hodgepodge lives next door to us. She doesn't like noise, children and dancing – which means she's not very keen on me!

I call Penelope and Priscilla Pinkpaws the terrible twins – because they are! They are spoilt and have the best of everything – and they're very, very sneaky!

12

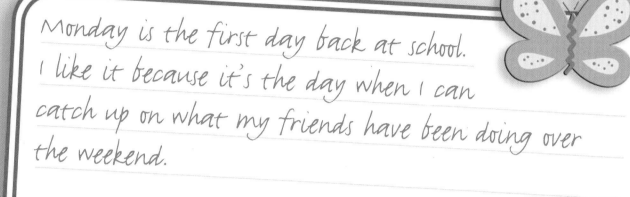

Monday is the first day back at school. I like it because it's the day when I can catch up on what my friends have been doing over the weekend.

Monday is washing day. It's a busy day for Mum, so I like to help when I get home from school. That means pegging all the wet washing out on the line in the garden. It's fun when the wind blows extra hard!

What do you do on Mondays? Why not write your name and fill in your own diary?

_____'s diary: Monday

The Costume Ball

There was going to be a grand Costume Ball in the village hall, and Angelina really wanted to go! "Please, Mum," she said. "Everyone's going!"

"If you're going as a queen and Dad's going as a king, why can't I be your princess?" said Angelina. "I promise I'll be good. Pleeeeeease?"

"No, I'm sorry, Angelina," said Mrs Mouseling. "The Costume Ball is for grown-ups, not little mouselings." Angelina stomped off. "It's just not fair!"

Later on Angelina told Alice what had happened. Her face was angry, but she had to smile when she and Alice tried on some of her dressing-up clothes.

"Oh, Alice!" said Angelina, as her friend tripped on the hem of her dress – and landed on top of her! They both rolled on to the floor, giggling.

Alice pulled at the dress. "You could fit both of us in this!" she laughed. Angelina nodded. "Yes," she said, then paused. "Yes, you could!"

That night Angelina's mum was dressed as a queen, but her dad was dressed as – a bee! There had been a bit of a mix-up at the costume shop!

When Mrs Hodgepodge arrived, Angelina and Alice groaned and pulled faces. She was the last person they wanted as their babysitter!

"I hope you're going to be good little mouselings for Mrs Hodgepodge?" said Mrs Mouseling. Angelina looked at Alice. "We'll try …" she said.

That night Angelina and Alice were glad when Mrs Hodgepodge sent them up to bed. They clutched their tummies and groaned.

"Urgh," said Angelina. "Supper was horrible!" Alice nodded. "Mrs Hodgepodge's smelly green cabbage jelly is the worst thing – yuck!"

When Angelina opened the bedroom window she could hear the music from the Costume Ball, and took Alice's paw in hers.

"Would you care to dance,
Miss Nimbletoes?" she asked.
Alice giggled as she answered
in her poshest voice. "I'd love
to, Miss Mouseling!"

They waltzed around,
round and round, faster and
faster, until they were dizzy.
Then Alice landed – ooof! –
in the dressing-up box!

As Angelina helped Alice
to her feet she pulled the long
dress from the box. It gave her
an idea. "Come on," she said.
"We're going to the Ball!"

"But what about Mrs
Hodgepodge?" said Alice.
"She's fast asleep downstairs,"
said Angelina. "We'll be back
before she wakes up."

Minutes later a new guest arrived at the Ball. It was Angelina, dressed in a long dress and a big hat, sitting on Alice's shoulders!

"Isn't it a wonderful party?" said a voice beside her. It was Miss Lilly! "Oh, yes, Miss Li … er … it's … er … unmissable!" said Angelina.

Angelina wanted to dance, but no one seemed to want to dance with her. Alice didn't mind – she was much more interested in the food table.

Angelina did dance a reel, but she was very heavy for Alice to carry around. Poor Alice! She stumbled, spun – and crashed into the food table!

Alice's head appeared beside Angelina's in the neck of the dress – and Mrs Hodgepodge arrived! "You naughty mouselings!" she said.

The next day, Angelina and Alice were back in the village hall. But this time they weren't dancing – they were scrubbing the floor as a punishment.

They were rubbing their sore paws when Mrs Mouseling arrived with some sandwiches. But why did she smile when they took big bites?

"Yuck!" said Alice, pulling a face. "What's in these sandwiches?" Angelina knew. "Urgh! It's Mrs Hodgepodge's green cabbage jelly!"

Angelina's picture

Angelina likes drawing and painting. Today she's painting a picture of – herself!

Would you like to draw a picture of Angelina and Alice? It's easy if you copy the lines square by square.

When your drawing is complete, colour it as neatly as you can. Copy the colours or choose ones you like, then write your name on the line.

Angelina and Alice by

Tuesday is my very, very favourite day of the week because it's the day when I have my dance class at Miss Lilly's ballet school.

She was so pleased with me this week! "Angelina darlink, you dance like a dream!" she said. You should have seen the Pinkpaws twins' faces! They were green with envy — as green as Mrs Hodgepodge's yucky cabbage jelly!

What do you do on Tuesdays? Why not write your name and fill in your own diary?

FLORENCE

's diary: Tuesday

SCHOOL

Alice's present

One day in school Alice handed Angelina a parcel. Inside was a lovely patchwork bag.

"I made it for you," said Alice. "It's to put your gym things in."

"It's beautiful!" said Angelina, hugging her best friend. "I love it! Thank you, thank you, Alice!"

"I didn't know it was your birthday," said Priscilla Pinkpaws.

"We'd have got you a present if we'd known," added Penelope, smirking.

"It's not my birthday," said Angelina.

"Best friends can give each other presents any time they like," said Alice.

"Yes," said Angelina, taking Alice's paw. "Come on, it's time for gym."

But the door of the gym was locked.

"Sorry, no gym today," said the teacher. "The equipment is too old. It's not safe for you to

use it. We're going to try to raise the money to pay for a new gym with a Fundraising Fair."

On the way home, Alice had an idea for the Fair.

"We could do a gymnastics show!" she said, doing a perfect cartwheel.

"Yes," said Angelina. "And William can collect the money!"

The Pinkpaws twins had an idea for the Fair, too. "We're going to sell things people

don't want any more," Priscilla told Mrs Mouseling when they called at the cottage.

"Yes, just put any things you don't want outside the front door, and we'll collect them later," added Penelope.

Later, Angelina was rushing out of the cottage on her way to practise with Alice when Mrs Mouseling reminded her that there were dishes to be done first.

Angelina sighed and put

down her gym bag by the front door – which is where Penelope and Priscilla found it! They picked it up and walked away, smiling slyly.

Alice was on the village green when the Pinkpaws twins walked by with some old books, a lamp – and Angelina's gym bag!

"What are you doing with that bag?" she asked.

"Selling it on our unwanted items stall," said

Priscilla with a smile.

"Shame, but I don't think Angelina wants your home-made gift," added Penelope.

When Angelina couldn't find her gym bag she made William promise not to tell Alice that it was lost and that her gym things were in it.

"Let's do ballet instead of gymnastics," she said to Alice.

"We're always doing ballet," said Alice. "You don't want to do gym because I'm better at it than you! You never

want to do things I'm good at!
You even hate that I'm good
at sewing!"

"What?" said Angelina.
"Alice, I …"

But before Angelina could
say anything else, Alice turned
and marched off.

The next day, Angelina
and William went to Alice's
house with a big bar of
chocolate. But as she knocked
on the door Angelina picked up
a ballet book that was lying on a

pile of old things.

"Alice left it out for the
Pinkpaws twins' unwanted
items stall," Mrs Nimbletoes
told her.

"But I gave this to Alice,"
said Angelina. "So that's what
she thinks of my present!"

Later on, Mrs Nimbletoes
talked to Alice. "Have you and
Angelina had an argument?"
she asked.

"She started it!" said Alice.
"She gave away my gym bag!"

"I think you should give her a chance to explain," said Mrs Nimbletoes.

"Oh, all right," said Alice.

She found Angelina and William practising.

When she heard Angelina say, "I just don't need friends like Alice," Alice picked up a hose Henry had been using to water the garden – and turned it on Angelina.

"And I don't need friends like you!" said Alice.

Angelina stamped her foot. "Good!"

A few days later the Fundraising Fair was set up on the village green.

The Pinkpaws were setting things out on their unwanted items stall.

Alice was warming up for her gymnastics display.

Angelina, William and Henry were getting ready for their ballet.

"Where's the bag for the

money, Henry?" said Angelina.

"Oops," said Henry. "I forgot it."

William gave Henry a penny. "See if you can buy one," he said.

"OK!" said Henry.

He came back carrying Angelina's gym bag!

"Where did you find it?" asked Angelina.

"You gave it to us," said Priscilla.

"I did not!" said Angelina.

"You did!" said Penelope. "You left it outside your door."

Angelina gasped. "So that's where it went!"

"It's worth more than a penny," said Priscilla, holding out her paw.

Angelina hugged the bag. "Yes, it's worth MUCH more than a penny!" she said. "MUCH, MUCH more!"

Alice had heard everything and went over to Angelina.

"I thought you didn't want the gym bag and gave it

away," she said.

Angelina hugged Alice. "Oh, Alice, I would never do that! Never!"

After the Fair Angelina gave Alice the big bar of chocolate.

"But it's not my birthday," said Alice.

"Well, best friends can give each other presents any time they like!" said Angelina.

Alice came round after school today and we dressed up in our tutus and ballet shoes and danced around like famous ballerinas.

When she had gone home I felt a bit daydreamy. I'll have to work hard, but I know my dream will come true one day. Then I'll be a big star, just like Miss Lilly!

What do you do on Wednesdays? Why not write your name and fill in your own diary?

_____ 's diary: Wednesday

Angelina needs your help!

"A mouseling can never have too many hair ribbons and pairs of ballet shoes! But they do have a habit of getting themselves lost! Can you help me find five ribbons and three pairs of ballet shoes in my bedroom?"

"A mouseling can never have too many ballet tutus, either! Will you colour in some new ones for me? Which do you think I'll like best?"

Angelina at the fair

It was the end of Miss Lilly's ballet class and for once the mouselings couldn't wait to take off their ballet shoes because the fair was in town.

"Just think, Alice," said Angelina happily. "In one hour we'll be riding on the biggest, scariest, fastest rollercoaster in all of Mouseland."

"I bet it's got a hundred loops," said Alice. "No, a thousand!" said Angelina. "A million!" said Alice as they rushed towards the door. "Come on, William!"

Angelina was leaving for the fair when Mrs Mouseling called her back. "You promised to look after Henry, remember?" she said. "I did?" said Angelina.

"Yes, you did," said Mrs Mouseling firmly. "But you can still go to the fair. You can take Henry with you." Angelina groaned. "Oh, all right then …"

Henry wanted a big blue balloon, but Angelina was saving her money to buy candyfloss later. She wanted to go on the rides with her friends.

Angelina lifted Henry into a rocking basket on the Big Wheel ride. But Henry didn't like it at all. "Stop! I feel sick!" he cried. "I want to get off. NOW!"

The Big Wheel stopped with a jolt and as the other riders watched, Angelina and a very green Henry got off. Angelina had never been so embarrassed!

Angelina and the others went to the Haunted House next. "I don't like it!" said Henry. "I'm scared of the dark." Angelina groaned. "Then close your eyes!"

William took Henry's hand and they went inside. It was dark, and when a bony skeleton popped out, William jumped and let go of Henry's hand.

In the dark, Henry walked towards a shape and took its hand. But it wasn't William – it was a giant hairy spider! "Aaah!" screamed Henry. "HEEELLLP!"

The lights went on and Henry and the others filed out of the Haunted House. They felt very silly. "I can't help it," said Henry. "I'm scared of spiders."

 **13**

 **14**

When William and Alice went on the Helter Skelter ride Angelina could only sit and watch. Can you guess why? Yes, Henry didn't like it.

When Henry asked if he could go on the little merry-go-round instead, Angelina sighed. "Do not say a word, Henry," she said. "Not a word."

 **15**

 **16**

William and Alice were very excited after the Helter Skelter. "Angelina, come on the Loop the Loop Rollercoaster with us," said Alice. "You HAVE to!"

Angelina looked at Henry. He shook his head. "I don't like rollercoasters," he said. Poor Angelina gritted her teeth. "Why am I not surprised?" she asked.

Just then a clown called out, "Clown show in ten minutes!" That gave Angelina an idea. "You like clowns, don't you, Henry?" she asked sweetly.

Minutes later Angelina, Alice and William were squealing and screaming on the rollercoaster ride. They liked it so much that they stayed on for another turn.

Henry was watching the clowns, but he was much more interested in a big blue balloon that floated past. He got up from his seat and followed it …

Eight thrilling rollercoaster rides later, Angelina and the others went to find Henry. But he was nowhere to be seen! "I have to find him," said Angelina.

They looked everywhere, but no one had seen Henry. "What am I going to do?" sobbed Angelina. "I was supposed to be looking after him."

Just then Angelina saw a big blue balloon float by – with a little mouseling chasing after it. "Henry?" she cried. "Yes, look, it's Henry!"

Henry was about to grab the balloon when Angelina scooped him up. He burst into tears as the balloon floated away. "My balloon! Waaaaahhhh!"

Soon after, Angelina and Henry – and a new balloon – were on the little merry-go-round. "I don't like candyfloss much anyway!" said Angelina.

Angelina's diary: Thursday

Mum asked me to babysit cousin Henry and my baby sister Polly after school. We had a lovely time. We sat in Dad's big cosy chair and I read them a story all about – guess what? – a little ballerina.

Henry can be a pain sometimes, but I love him really.

Polly's so sweet! I bet she'll be a real chatterbox when she learns to talk – just like her big sister!

What do you do on Thursdays? Why not write your name and fill in your own diary?

_____'s diary: Thursday

The royal banquet

One afternoon when Doctor Tuttle came to tea he told the Mouseling family all about the hot-air balloon ride he was going on that weekend.

Then Miss Lilly arrived. "Darrrrlink Angelina, I have the most wonderful news," she cried. "Of course, we will have to stay the night, and ..."

Mr Mouseling stared. "Er, what are you talking about?" he asked. "Angelina has been chosen to dance at the royal palace banquet!" said Miss Lilly.

On Saturday Angelina was practising for her visit to the palace, curtsying to her doll and teddy, when Mrs Mouseling came in with her new dress.

"Oh, Mum, it's the most beautiful dress ever!" she said. Mrs Mouseling smiled, and helped Angelina pack it into her bag. "Hurry, you'll be late!"

Angelina sat beside Miss Lilly on the train. She was wearing an amazing outfit – and she had the biggest suitcase in the world!

Miss Lilly told Angelina about how she and Queen Seraphina had been the very best of friends when they were young mouselings.

Hills, trees and fields rushed by as Miss Lilly talked of how they had played, rolling all the way down Stilton Hill in the mud. Angelina listened, entranced.

Miss Lilly was asking a waiter for hot chocolate drinks when there was a loud SCREECH! and a JOLT! and the train came to a sudden stop.

Minutes later, Miss Lilly and Angelina were trudging through a field of tall corn. "We cannot wait six hours for a new train!" said Miss Lilly. "Come, darrlink!"

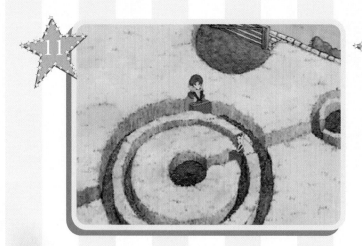

Angelina looked around. "Do you know the way?" she asked. "Well, no, but we will find the gate, then the road – and then the palace!" said Miss Lilly.

After walking for hours they did find a gate – into another field. "Keep going," said Miss Lilly as she slid down a wet slope – into a river! "Help!" she cried.

A fisherman called Scampi gave them a lift in his little boat. But he crashed into the bank and – SPLASH! – Miss Lilly's suitcase fell into the water!

At last Scampi got them to dry land. But there were no taxis. "My mate Zoomer will lend you his motorbike," said Scampi. "But can you ride one?" said Angelina.

"It's easy!" said Miss Lilly as she zoomed along. Miss Lilly did know how to ride the big motorbike, but she didn't know how to turn corners or stop!

When Miss Lilly went round a bend she ran off the road and into a hedge. Angelina was thrown off. "Where are you, Miss Lilly?" she cried.

"In … the … hedge," said Miss Lilly. Angelina pulled her out – into a muddy puddle! Poor Miss Lilly! She sighed and took off her crash helmet.

There was something else in the puddle – Angelina's dress, all ripped and torn. She burst into tears. "Oh, no! My beautiful dress," she sobbed.

Miss Lilly was giving Angelina a big hug to make her feel better when they heard Doctor Tuttle's voice. "Need a lift?" he asked from up in the hot-air balloon.

Queen Seraphina and Princess Valentine could not believe it when the balloon landed at the palace. Neither could Angelina. "We made it!"

"This is my little star," said Miss Lilly, and Angelina curtsyed. But as she did so she saw her dirty, ripped clothes and said, "How can I dance like this?"

"Come with me, Angelina," said Princess Valentine. Then the queen turned to Miss Lilly. "And you come with me, my muddy, dear friend," she said.

Soon, Miss Lilly was at the banquet dressed like a queen and Angelina was on stage. She danced better than she had ever danced before.

"Magnificent!" said Miss Lilly as the audience clapped and cheered. "You were right, Lilly," said the queen. "Angelina is a real star – just like you!"

What's different?

It's always an extra-busy time at Miss Lilly's ballet school when there's a new show to prepare for!

1

These pictures look the same, but if you look very carefully you'll see that there are five things that are different in picture 2. Can you spot them all?

2

Mum's famous for her Cheddar Pie! It's my very favourite supper in all the world and tonight she let me help her make it! I do like cooking, but not half as much as dancing!

Dad stopped playing his fiddle because he said the smell was so good that he couldn't keep his mind on the music. I think it was one of his jokes!

What do you do on Fridays? Why not write your name and fill in your own diary?

I on d 's diary: Friday

Alliahl Jo come round.

Angelina and Grandma

Miss Lilly was handing out the costumes for her new Sleeping Beauty ballet. There were Wicked Fairy costumes for Priscilla and Penelope Pinkpaws and a knight's costume for William.

"And now … Angelina," said Miss Lilly, opening a cardboard dress box and taking out a beautiful old tutu. "I wore this when I danced the Sleeping Beauty many years ago."

"This was your tutu?" asked Angelina.

"Yes, darrlink, and now you may wear it," said Miss Lilly. "But you must look after it carefully because it is full of memories."

"I will, Miss Lilly," said Angelina. "I promise."

That night Angelina was wearing the old tutu when Mrs Mouseling went up to say goodnight.

"That seam is starting to split," said Mrs Mouseling.

"Can you fix it, Mum?" asked Angelina. "The dress

rehearsal is tomorrow."

"I'll do it first thing in the morning," said Mrs Mouseling.

But in the night Angelina's mum got some exciting news. Her sister was having a baby, and she and Mr Mouseling drove off to look after her.

Angelina went to stay with Grandma and Grandpa, but she didn't feel tired any more. She wanted to tell her grandparents all about the new ballet.

She put on Miss Lilly's tutu and acted out the story for

them. "The Wicked Fairies make me prick my finger and I fall down – like this! But I'm not dead, just fast asleep!"

"Which is what we should be," said Grandpa. "Time for bed, Angelina."

Grandma yawned. "Yes, we've all got a big day tomorrow. There's your rehearsal, and we're having a birthday party in the garden for Mrs Twinkle. You can help."

"I'd love to," said Angelina, leaping to her feet.

R-I-I-I-P!

Oh, no, there was a big tear in the old tutu!

"What am I going to do?" said Angelina.

"I'll mend it tomorrow," said Grandma.

In the morning Grandma was getting things ready for the party when Angelina handed her her sewing basket.

"I'll do it when everything else is done," said Grandma.

"Right, I'll lay the table

while Grandpa collects the cake," said Angelina.

When Angelina went to find Grandma she was in the kitchen making cheese sauce.

"You stir the sauce while I cut some flowers," said Grandma. "Don't let it go lumpy."

Angelina was still worried about her costume. "Then will you fix my tutu?" she asked.

"We'll see … we'll see," said Grandma.

When Grandma went back into the kitchen Angelina was practising her steps – and the cheese sauce was lumpy. "I'll have to make some more," said Grandma. "And it's going to rain, so we need to move everything inside."

"I'll do it," said Angelina. She worked hard and soon everything was in place.

"Now will you do my tutu?" asked Angelina as there was a knock on the door.

"They're here already!" said Grandma.

Grandpa showed Mrs Twinkle to her chair – the chair with Angelina's tutu on it!

Angelina snatched it up just in time, but – CRASH! – she dropped the vase of flowers she was carrying.

"Angelina, take your tutu to your room," said Grandma.

"But you haven't fixed it yet!" whispered Angelina.

"I can't do it NOW, can I?" whispered Grandma.

"I'll go and make us all a nice cup of tea," said Grandpa.

As Angelina went into her bedroom there was a flash of lightning and a loud clap of thunder. She looked out of the window as heavy rain began to fall and groaned.

"Oh, no!" said Angelina. "The cake's still on the table outside!"

Angelina rescued the cake and put it on the dining room table.

"It's ruined!" said Grandma. "Why did you leave it outside, Angelina?"

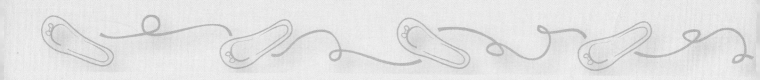

"I didn't!" said Angelina.

"I told you to bring everything inside," said Grandma crossly.

"I did!" said Angelina.

"No you didn't," said Grandma. "You were too busy worrying about your tutu. Please go to your room."

Grandma showed Grandpa the cake. "Angelina left it out in the rain," she said.

"No, I did," said Grandpa.

"Oh, I thought it was

Angelina," said Grandma. "I must go and talk to her …"

But Angelina wasn't in her room. She had climbed out of the window!

"Don't worry," said Grandpa. "We'll find her."

Angelina walked all the way to ballet school. By the time she got there she was wet, tired – and very cross indeed.

"I helped Grandma all morning so she'd have time to sew the tutu," Angelina told Miss Lilly. "Then she said I'd left the cake out in the rain. It's just not fair!"

Miss Lilly pinned the tutu together with safety pins. "There. Now shall we call to let them know you're safe?"

"I suppose so …" said Angelina.

The Sleeping Beauty rehearsal was almost over when Grandma and Grandpa arrived. They watched the last scene as William woke Angelina with a gentle kiss.

"I'm so sorry, Angelina," said Grandma.

"Me too," said Angelina.

Later that day Grandma sewed up the tear in Angelina's tutu as she acted out the story – with Grandpa as the Handsome Prince.

When the phone rang it was Mrs Mouseling with some news for Angelina.

"Auntie Amanda's had a baby boy!" said Angelina. Then she paused as she listened to her mum. "But why do I have to come home today, Mum? I want to stay a bit longer. We're having SUCH a lovely time! Grandma's mended my tutu – and Grandpa makes a lovely Handsome Prince!"

Angelina's diary: saturday

Saturday is pocket money day. I always cycle into the village with Alice to spend my pennies in Mrs Thimble's shop.

She doesn't mind how long it takes us to decide what to buy. We're in there for hours sometimes! This week I chose new ballet shoe ribbons and I had enough left over for a lollipop. How great is that?!

What do you do on Saturdays? Why not write your name and fill in your own diary?

_____'s diary: saturday

Treasure tandems

1

It was the day of the Chipping Cheddar Treasure Hunt and all the mouselings were ready to race off on tandems. There was a shiny new one for the winners.

2

Mr Pedalpaws, who runs the bicycle shop, explained the rules. "You must solve all the clues then race to the finishing line. Ready, steady, GO!"

3

Angelina and Alice raced away. So did Priscilla and Penelope. But William and Henry were left behind. Henry's little legs didn't reach the pedals!

4

Alice tried to solve the first clue. "Old am I, an umbrella tree, in my sweet-smelling shade the next clue will be. Mmm. I bet that's the Old Cedar Tree."

Angelina and Alice hurried to the tree, but the Pinkpaws passed them and Penelope's hair ribbon came undone. It ended up over Angelina's eyes!

She didn't see the bend, and she and Alice crashed into a bush. "Those Pinkpaws!" said Angelina, pulling leaves from her fur. "We've got to catch them."

Priscilla and Penelope found the next clue on a clipboard at the Old Cedar Tree. When she had read the clue, Priscilla threw the board up into the tree!

When Angelina and Alice got to the tree they couldn't find the clue. "They've probably hidden it," said Angelina, looking up into the branches. "Yes, there it is!"

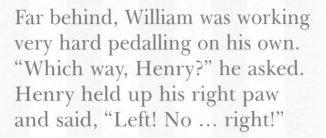

Far behind, William was working very hard pedalling on his own. "Which way, Henry?" he asked. Henry held up his right paw and said, "Left! No … right!"

They got to the Old Cedar Tree as Angelina was reading the clue. "To sail a boat or have a splash, to my far left bank you must pedal a dash."

"Millers Pond!" said William and Alice, and they all pedalled off. The Pinkpaws were there before them, but couldn't solve the clue. "Stuck?" said Angelina.

She read out the clue. "When you reach this stone, you'll have travelled one mile, you'll find the next clue on the old wooden stile." Alice said, "I know!"

She whispered to Angelina, and they pedalled off. "What shall we do?" asked Penelope. "Follow them of course!" said Priscilla. "Get pedalling!"

Angelina and Alice raced along as fast as they could, but the Pinkpaws were still right behind them. "I'll show them!" said Angelina.

She steered towards a path on the left, but turned right at the very last moment. The twins ended up – GLOOP! – in a huge muddy puddle.

The next clue was on the stile by the old Milestone. It said "Near this old stone mouse, both brave and wise, at the top of the hill you'll find first prize".

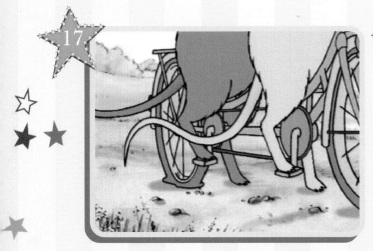

"The statue of the old mouse on Mouseborough Hill!" said Angelina. She and Alice started to climb the hill when – POP! – they got a puncture in their tyre!

By the time Angelina mended the puncture and they got back on the tandem the Pinkpaws arrived. The two tandem teams raced neck and neck up the hill.

Priscilla bumped Angelina so hard that she had to brake. The Pinkpaws wobbled and ran down the hill. "They're heading for the river!" cried Alice.

Angelina took off after them. She tried to grab their tandem, but it hit a log and they flew up into the air, landing in the river with a huge SPLASH!

Angelina took the bicycle pump in one paw and Alice's paw in the other. Alice grasped a tree and Angelina leaned out over the water. "Grab this!"

Soon Priscilla and Penelope were on dry land again, but they were very wet. "One of us can still win!" said Angelina. "Race you to the top!" said Priscilla.

The twins raced off up the hill and crossed the finishing line just ahead of Angelina and Alice. "Where's our prize then?" asked Penelope.

Angelina smiled and pointed to where Mr Pedalpaws was handing the shiny new tandem to – Henry and William! Even the Pinkpaws had to laugh!

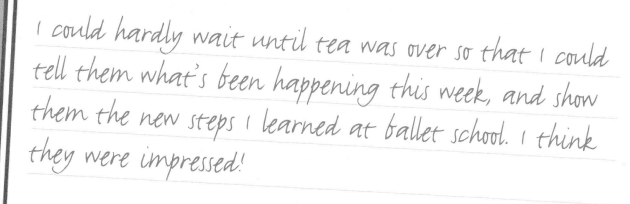

Sunday is the day when Grandma and Grandpa come to visit. Mum always makes cheese puffs and special little cakes with icing on top for tea.

I could hardly wait until tea was over so that I could tell them what's been happening this week, and show them the new steps I learned at ballet school. I think they were impressed!

What do you do on Sundays? Why not write your name and fill in your own diary?

_____'s diary: Sunday

_____

_____

_____

_____

_____

_____

How well do you know Angelina?

Try answering these questions to find out how much you know about Angelina Ballerina and her friends. The answers are at the bottom of page 69.

1 Angelina's baby sister is called Molly. True or false?

2 In the story "Treasure tandems" on page 60, who started the tandem race and gave William and Henry their prize?

3 What is the name of the Chipping Cheddar doctor?
Is it   a. Doctor Pickle
         b. Doctor Tuttle or
         c. Doctor Tickle?

4 In the story "Angelina at the fair" on page 34, who was scared of going on all the rides?

5 Mrs Podgepaws lives next door to Angelina. True or false?

6 In the story "The royal banquet" on page 42, what was the name of the princess who gave Angelina one of her dresses to wear?

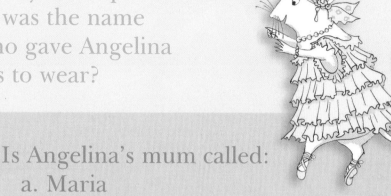

7 Is Angelina's mum called:
 a. Maria
 b. Marigold or
 c. Matilda?

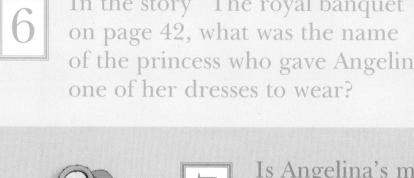

8 In the story "The Costume Ball" on page 14, what was in the sandwiches Mrs Mouseling brought for Angelina and Alice?

9 What is William's last name? Is it Longtail or Shortail?

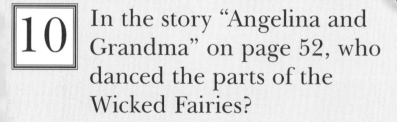

10 In the story "Angelina and Grandma" on page 52, who danced the parts of the Wicked Fairies?

Answers:
1. False, her name is Polly; 2. False, it's Mrs Hodgepodge who lives next door; 3. b. Doctor Tuttle 4. Henry 5. False, it's Mr Pedalpaws; 6. Valentine; 7. c. Matilda; 8. green cabbage jelly; 9. Longtail; 10. Penelope and Priscilla Pinkpaws.

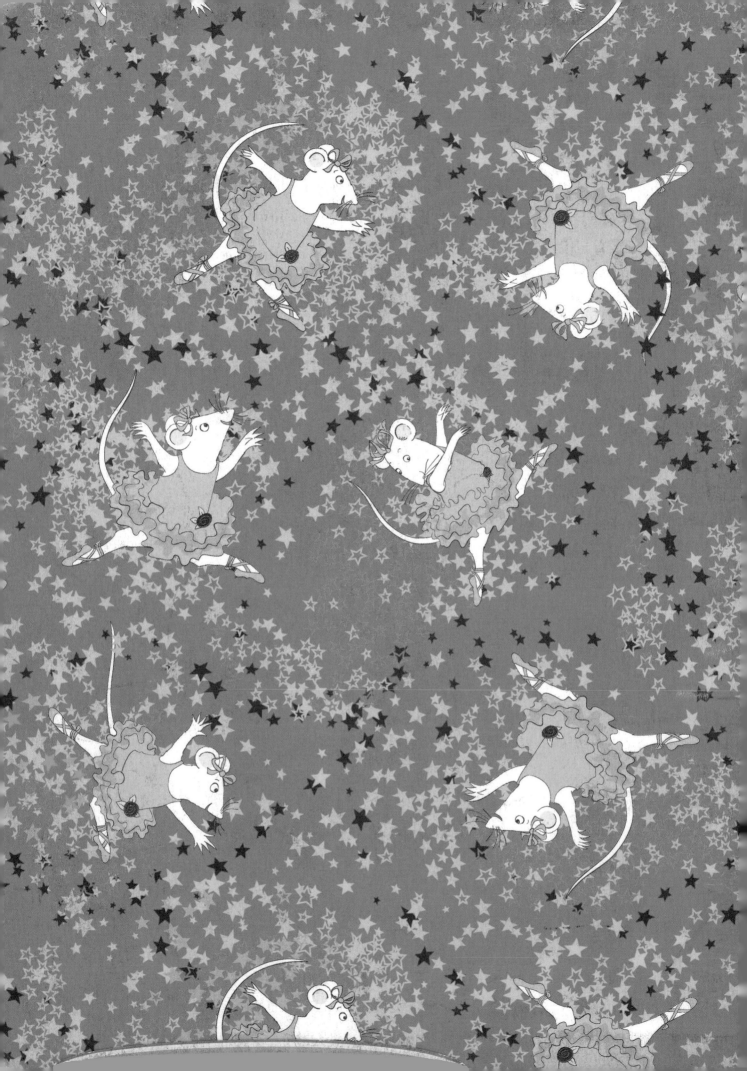